The Tiger Cub's First Words

By: Mei Y. Li
Illustrated by: Mei Y. Li,
John O'Hickey, and Edward O'Hickey

For my son, Edward, and his cousin Emilia, our water tigress.

This is a work of fiction. Names, characters, places, and incidents are either the product of the author's imagination or are used fictitiously. Any resemblance to actual persons or animals, living or dead, events, or locales is entirely coincidental.

All rights reserved. No part of this book may be reproduced, distributed, or transmitted in any form or by any means, including photocopying, recording, or other electronic or mechanical methods, without the prior written permission of the publisher, except in the case of brief quotations embodied in critical reviews and certain other noncommercial uses permitted by copyright law.

Copyright © 2022 by Mei Y. Li
First paperback edition January 2022
ISBN: 9798403361798 (Paperback)
Book written and designed by Mei Y. Li
Illustrated by Edward O'Hickey, John O'Hickey, and Mei Y. Li
Edited by Anna Bing, Linda Kow, and Amber Reed

Special thanks to Farrah Henry, Andria Lam, Deborah Ouderkirk, Purbita Saha, and Ricardo Serrano for your wonderings, suggestions, and support.

Independently Published
Montclair, N.J.

水

Shuǐ = Water

"Roar!!!" said Shuǐ.

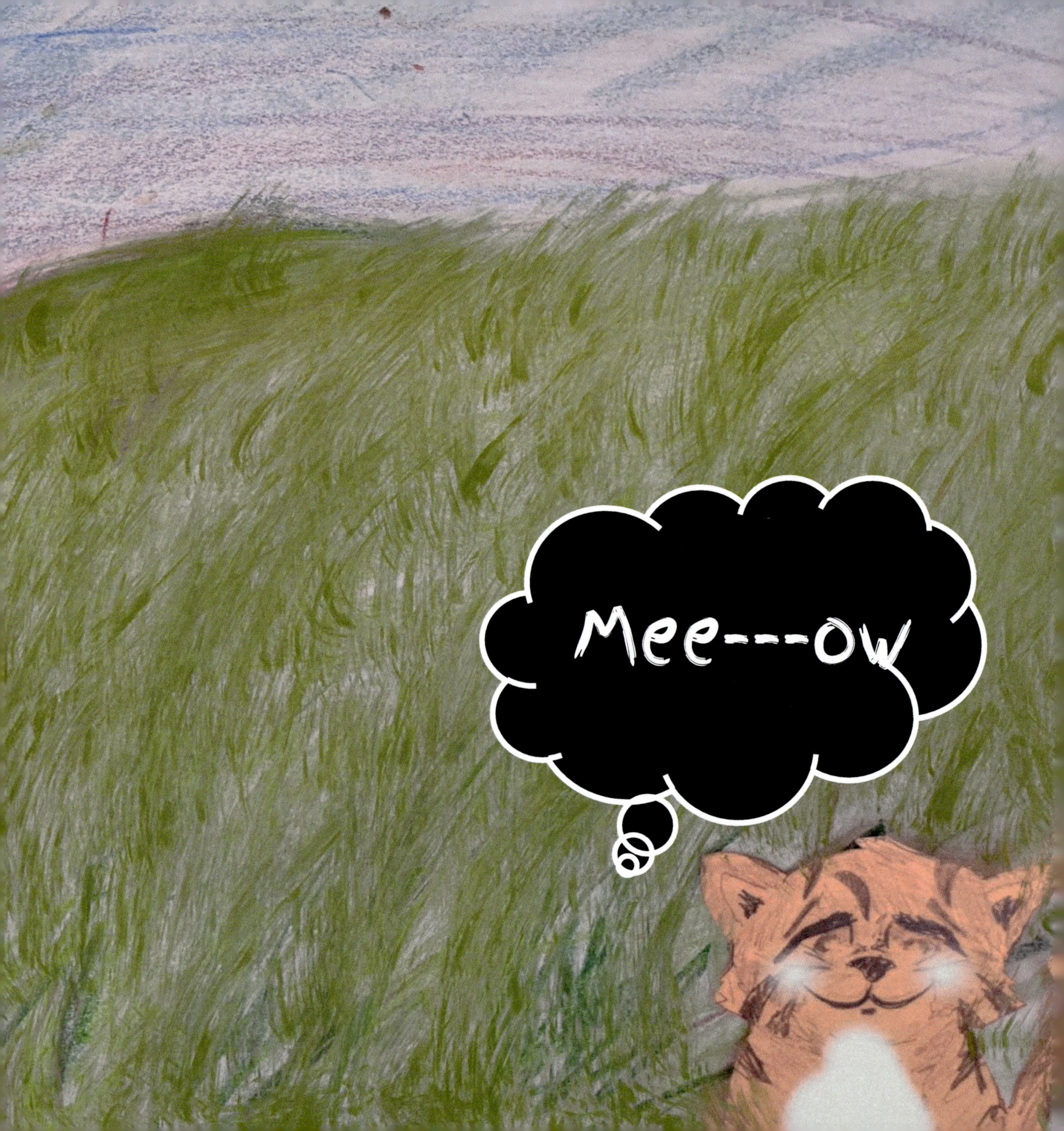
Mee---ow

Wait, thought Shuǐ. That was a lion's roar; too loud for a tiger.

Was it Meow? Yes, tigers meow, thought Shuǐ.

"Mee-ow," said Shuǐ with confidence.

Cousin Kitty

Shuǐ looked over at her mama's encouraging smile and her brother's confused eyes just as she remembered

that her cousins, the kittens meow, **not tigers**.

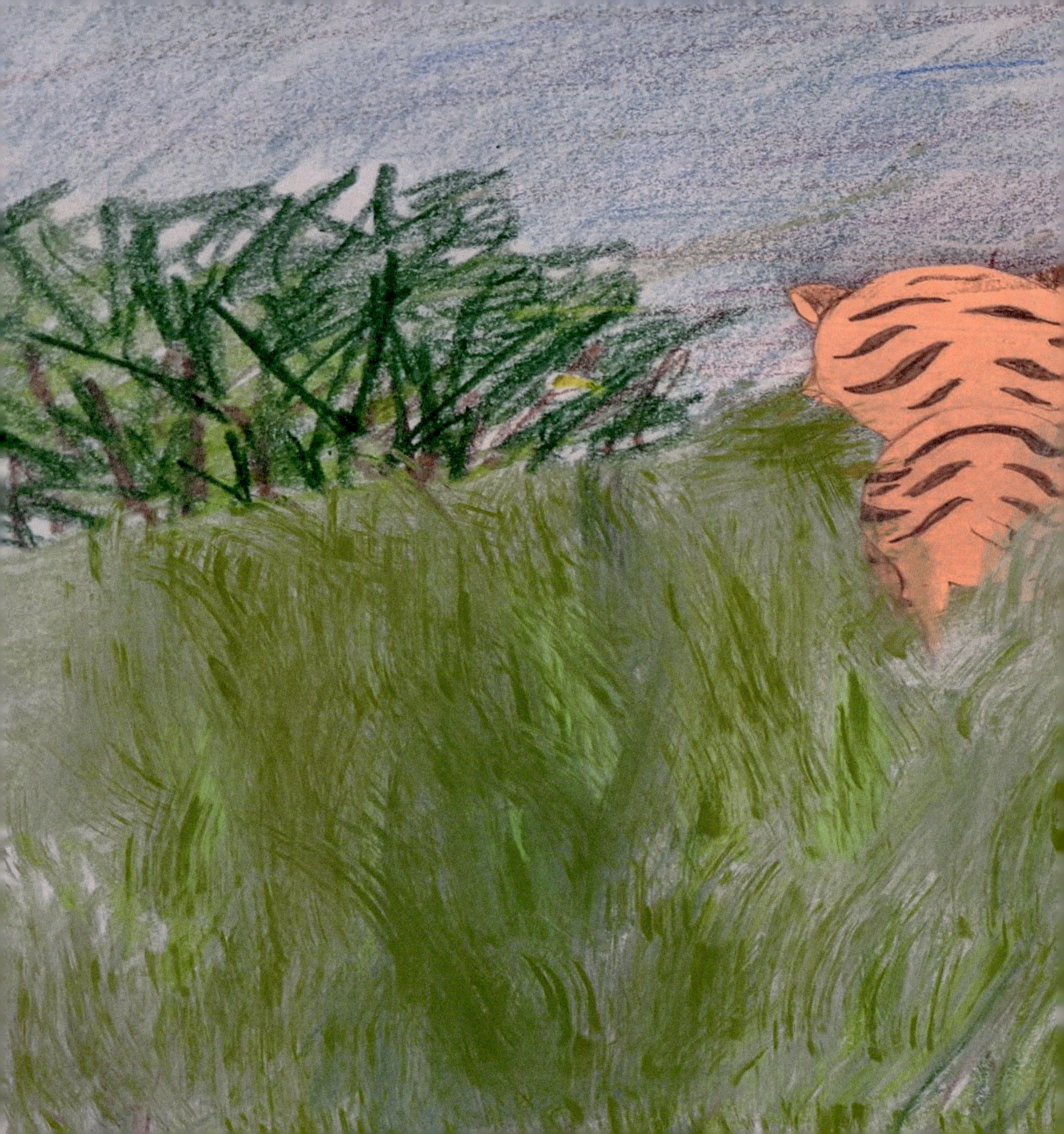

Determined to find the perfect first word for a tiger cub, Shuǐ walked.

Deep in thought, Shuǐ did not notice that she had wandered farther away from the grasslands - into the forest.

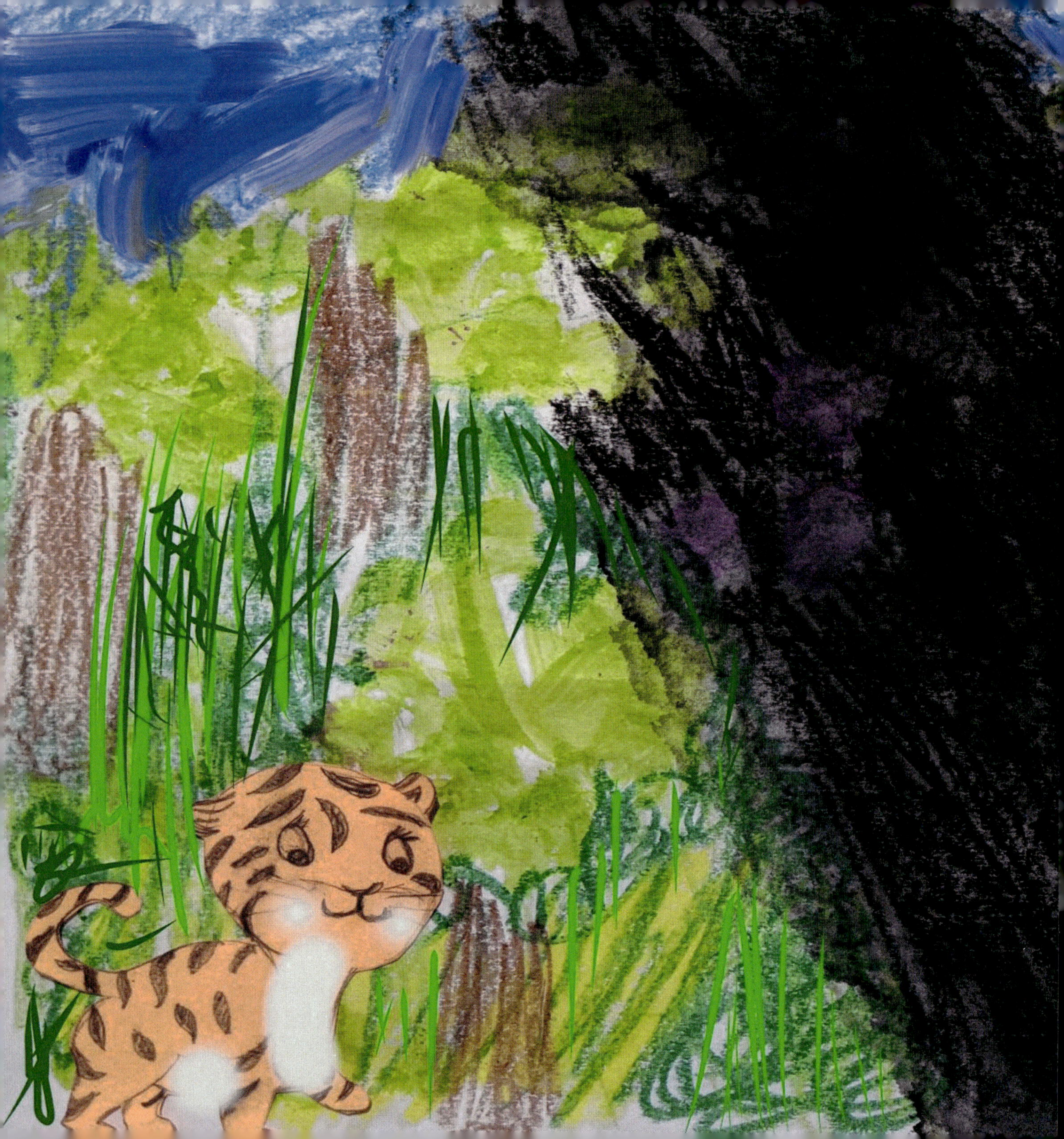

As she walked farther
    and deeper into the forest,
        a black river appeared.

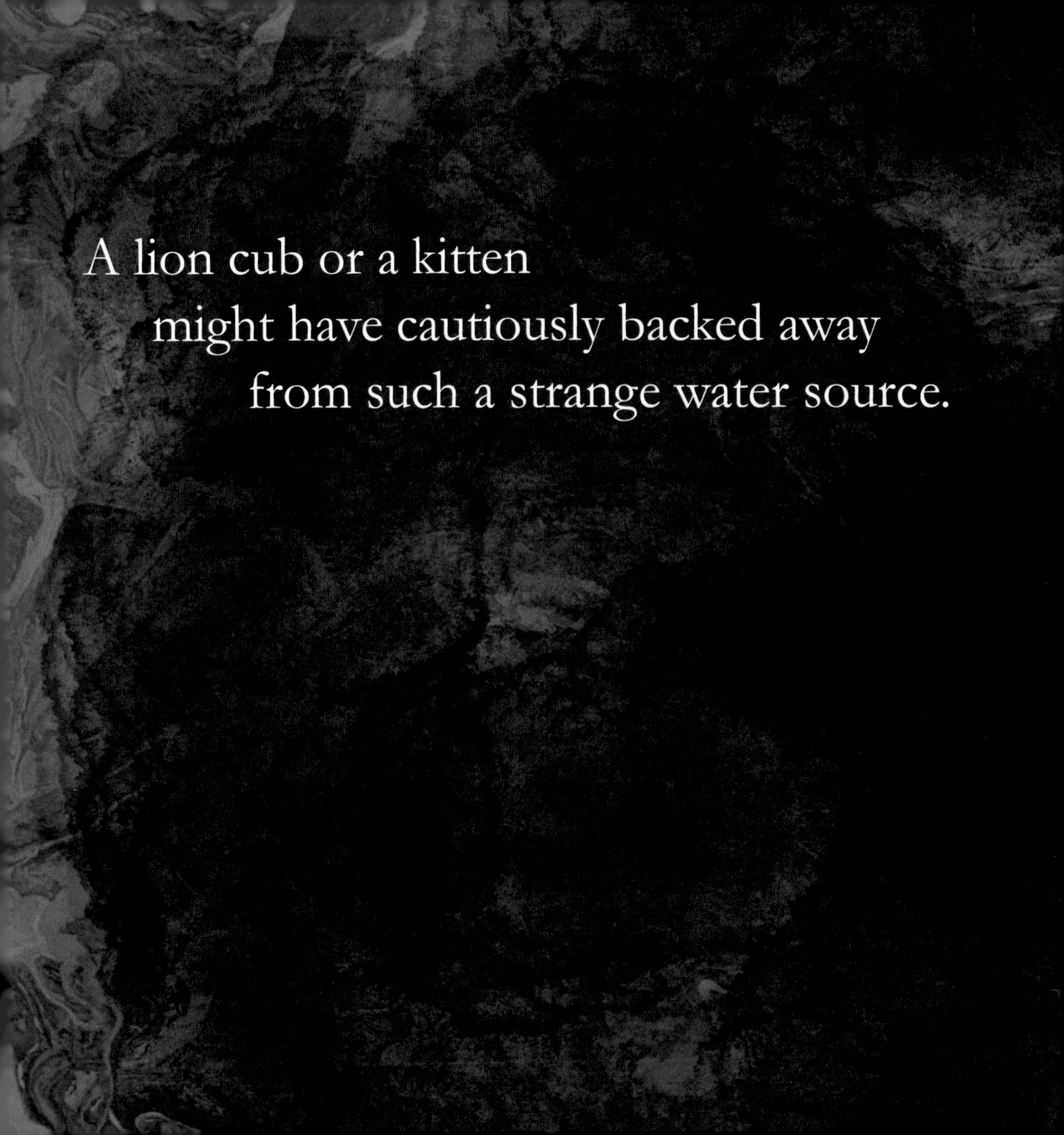

A lion cub or a kitten
   might have cautiously backed away
      from such a strange water source.

NOT Shuĭ.

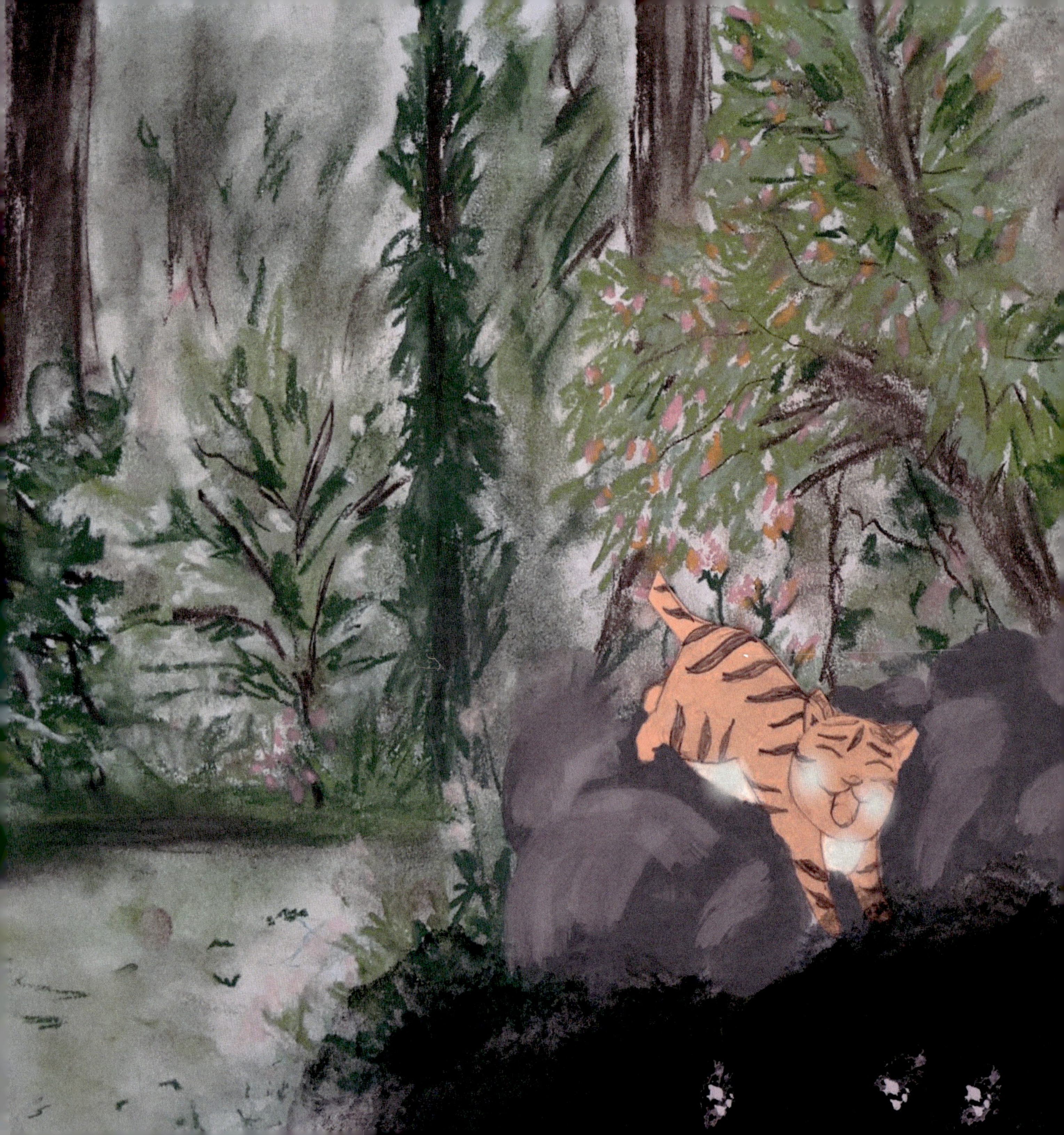

Shuǐ's eyes lit up.

With one paw *forward*

and then another,

Shuǐ ran

and……

dove into **the river!**

Shuǐ swam

deeper
and

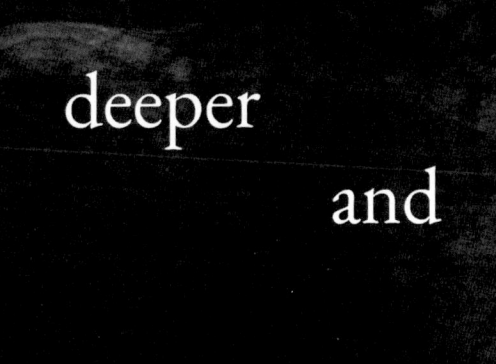

deeper

exploring
the wonder
of the black river.

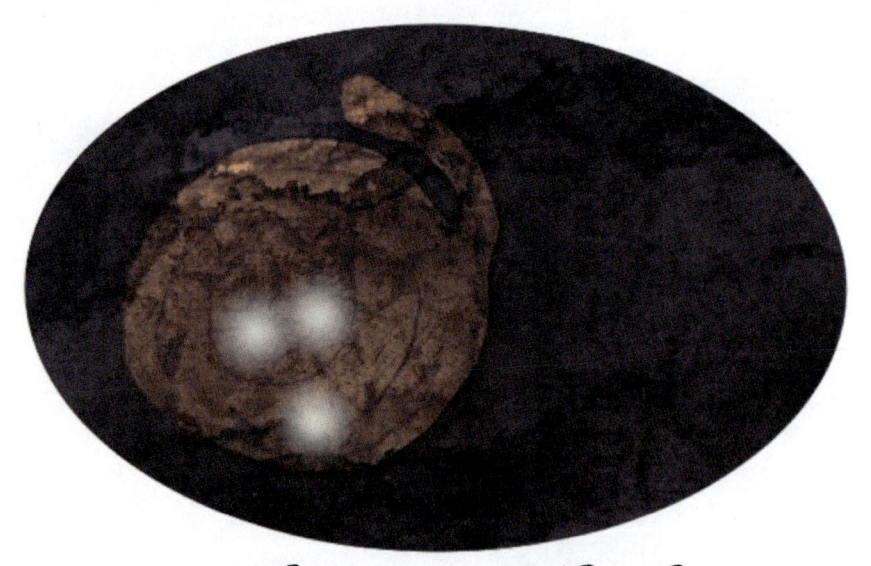

She twirled,

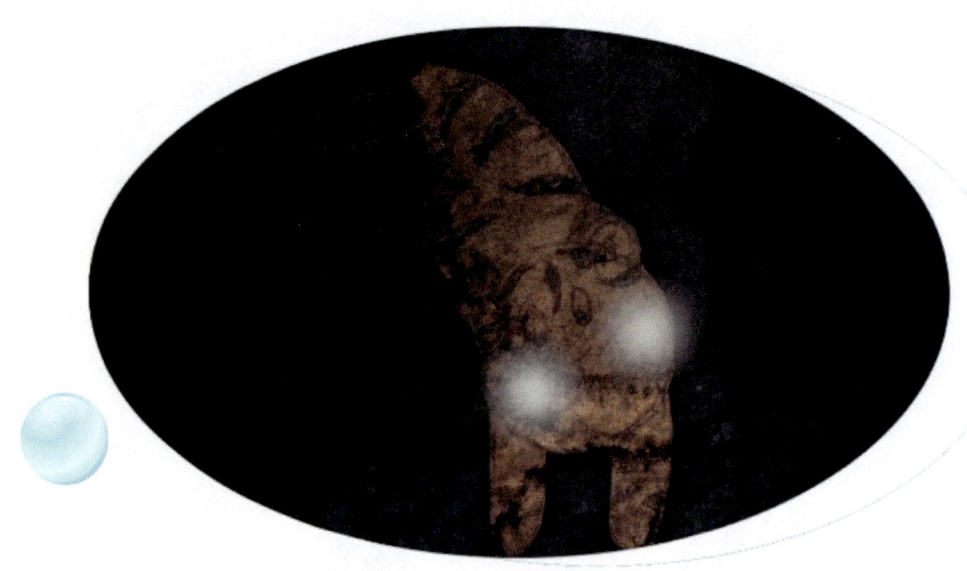

she flipped,

and she bounced

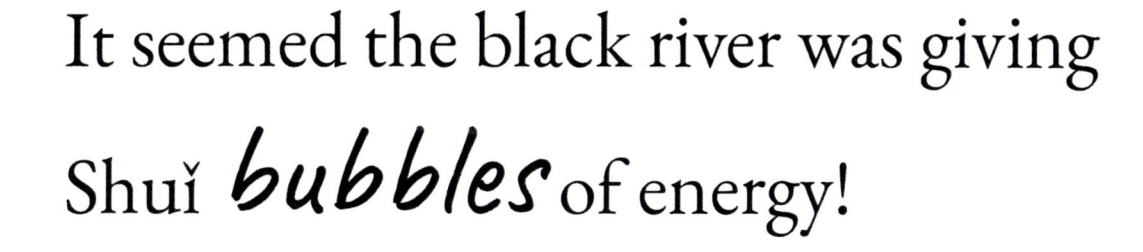

on **all** *the bubbles in the water.*

It seemed the black river was giving Shuǐ **bubbles** of energy!

BoiNG...

BoiNG...

BoiNG

... she could not stop bouncing!!!

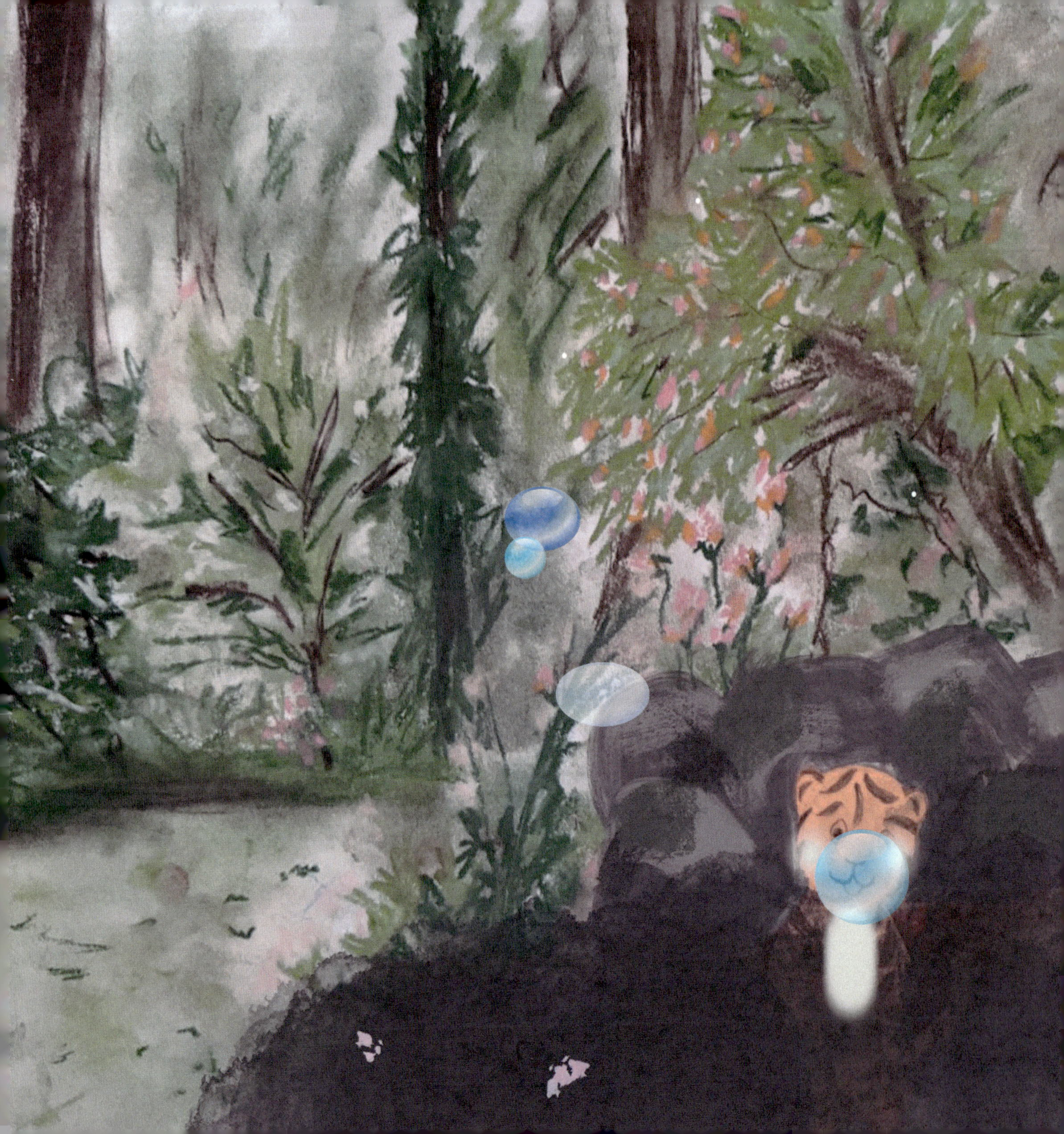

Out of the black water
bounced Shuǐ

and out of her mouth
came a…..

WATER BUBBLE!

Chuff

A babble of bouncing bubbles and a short **chuff** sound rang as Shuǐ bounced off a rock.

ROARR

Gprumf

Shuǐ bounced on the side of a tree trunk. A **Gprumf** sound similar to a horse's snort came out of her bubbling mouth.

Then another bounce, this time on top of a shrub! Out of her bouncing bubbling mouth came a tiger's **ROAR** that can freeze any creature in sight.

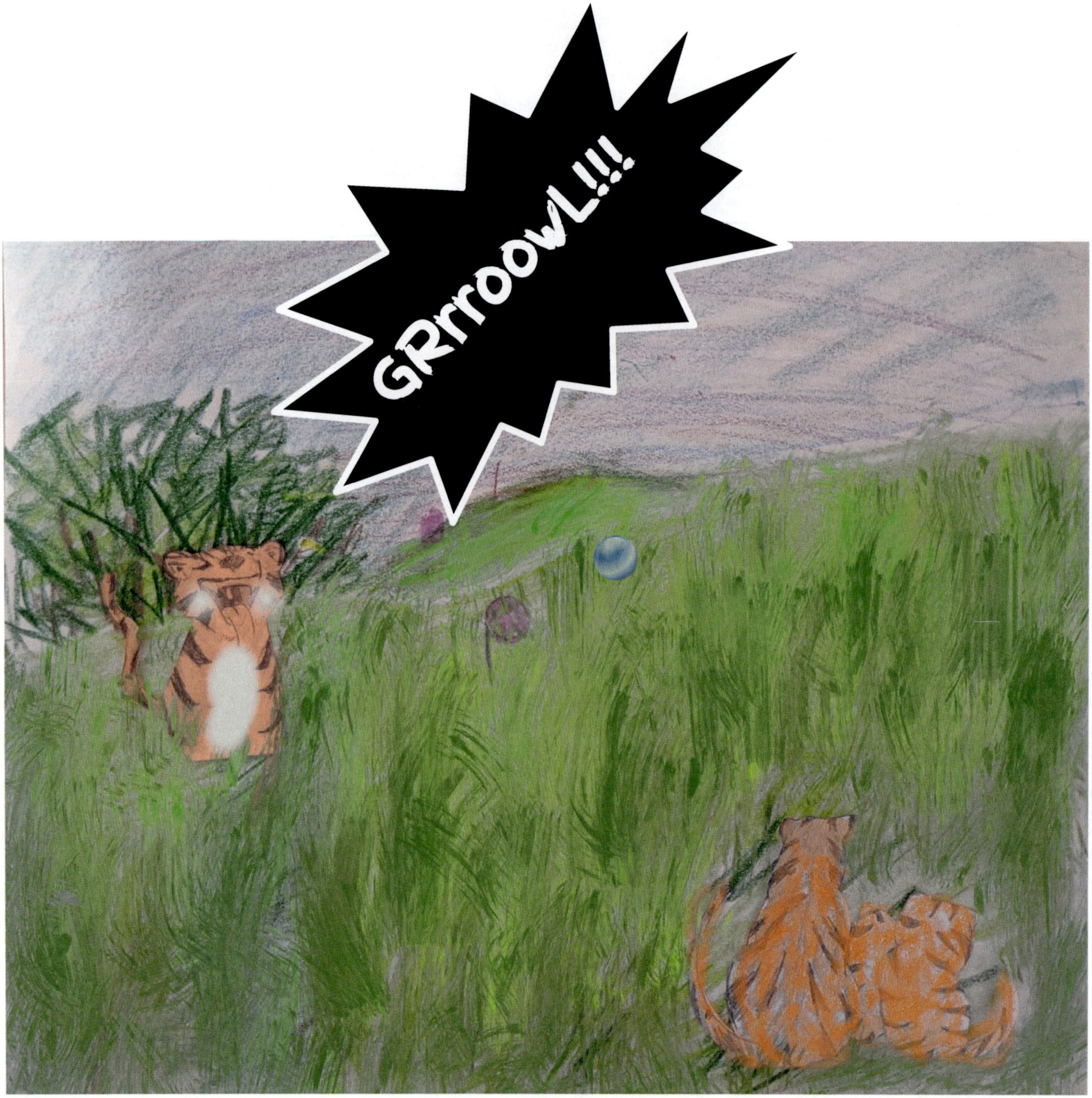
GRrroowL!!!

A final big bounce sent Shuǐ out onto the grasslands, right in front of her tiger mama and tiger siblings.

Shuǐ **GROWLed** as she plopped off her babbling bouncing bubble.

The tigers looked at Shuǐ with delight and **GROWLed** back in greeting.

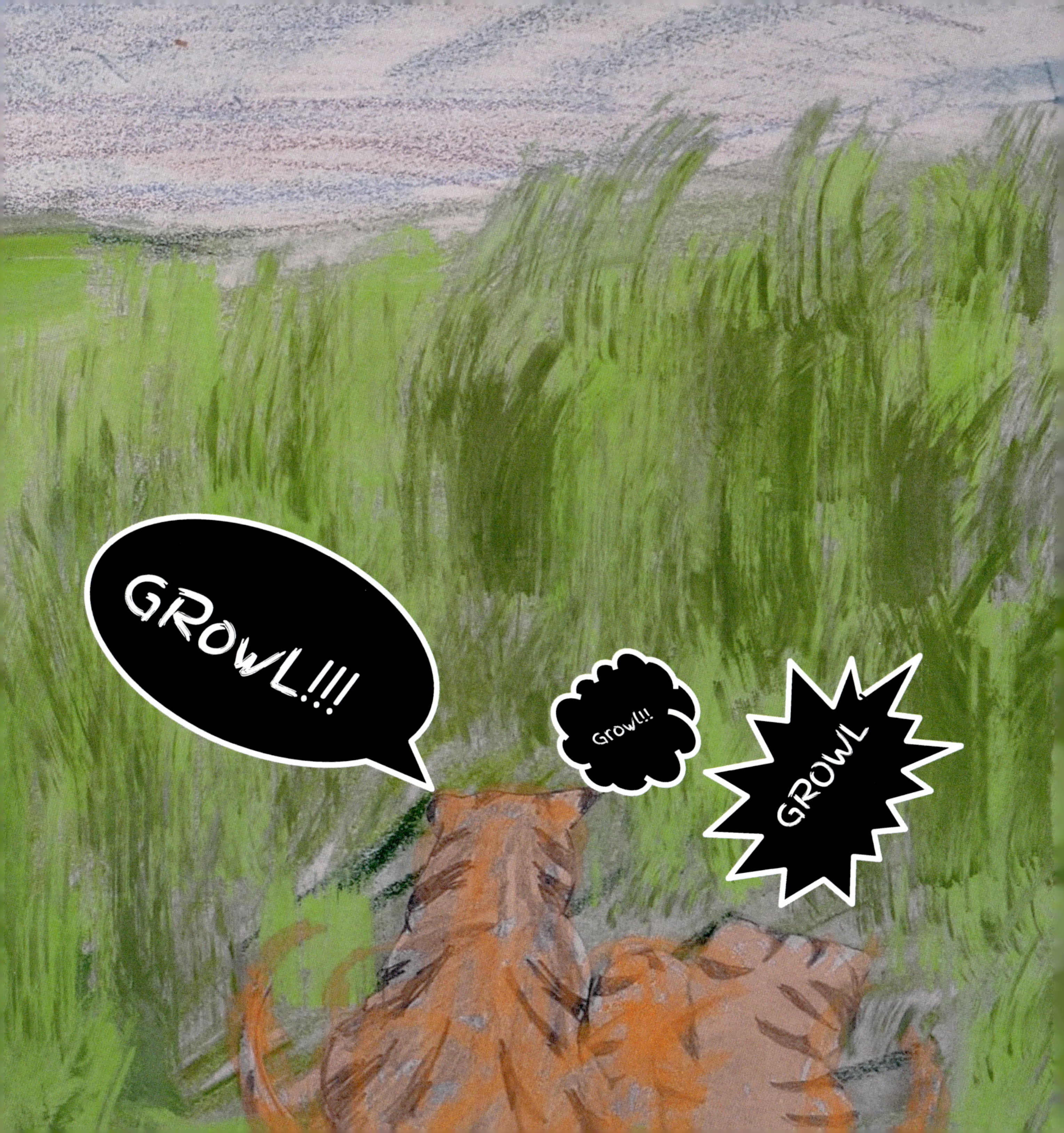
GROWL!!!
Growl!!
GROWL

*Like Shuǐ the tiger cub,
connect with yourself
and darkened waters
will become bubbles
that help you rise
to the top.*

Tiger Fun Facts

- Tigers can make many sounds including chuffling, growling, gurgling, grunting, and roaring. They do not purr or meow.

- Humans can hear frequencies from 20 hertz to 20,000 hertz but tigers can produce sounds below 20 hertz. This low-pitched sound can travel through forests and mountains.

- A tiger's scary roar has the power to stop prey in their tracks.

- Young tigers stay with their mothers until seventeen to twenty-four months of age. During this time, they play with their siblings and need their mother to help get food.

- Tigers spend most of their time by themselves, unlike lions who travel in a pride.

- Tigers are mainly active at night and are powerful swimmers.

ScienceDaily. (2000, December 29). *The secret of a tiger's roar*. ScienceDaily. Retrieved January 15, 2022, from https://www.sciencedaily.com/releases/2000/12/001201152406.htm

Tigers. SeaWorld Parks & Entertainment. (n.d.). Retrieved January 15, 2022, from https://seaworld.org/animals/all-about/tiger/ .

About Lunar New Year

- "Lunar New Year, also called Spring Festival, is the most important holiday in China. The festival is also celebrated in **Vietnam** (where it's known as Tet), **North and South Korea** (where it's known as Solnal) and **Tibet** (where it is called Losar)."

- "Oracle bones inscribed with astronomical records indicate that **the [lunar] calendar existed as early as 14th century B.C.**, when the Shang Dynasty was in power."

- "In Chinese element theory, each zodiac sign is associated with one of the five elements: Wood, Fire, Earth, Gold (Metal), and Water."

- "The year 2022 is slated to be the **year of the water tiger.** The tiger is known as the king of all beasts in China and the zodiac is associated with *strength, exorcising evils and bravery.*"

History.com Editors. (2010, February 4). *Lunar New Year 2022*. History.com. Retrieved January 15, 2022, from https://www.history.com/topics/holidays/chinese-new-year

Chinese zodiac tigers of 5 elements: Characters, destinies. 5 Elements, Character, and Destiny Analysis for People Born in a Year of the Tiger. (n.d.). Retrieved January 16, 2022, from https://www.chinahighlights.com/travelguide/chinese-zodiac/five-lements-character-destiny-analysis-tiger.htm

Suggested Discussion Prompts and Activities

- Find literary devices like Onomatopoeia, Repetition, and Alliteration. Read them out loud.

- What did Shuǐ want in the beginning of the story and how was this resolved by the end of the story?

- How would you describe Shui's character based on her feelings, thoughts, what she says, and her actions?

- Retell the story using sequence words, making sure to identify 5 important events in the story. (First,.. Then,.. . Next,... After that,... Eventually,... At the end,..)

- Choose one detail about tigers or Lunar New Year and research 5 to 8 facts about that detail. Create a presentation - powerpoint, video, diagram, board game, one pager, movie poster, or mobile museum.

- Illustrate a scene or event of choice with members of your family. Each member is allowed to add onto what the previous member contributed. May use as many mediums as you see fit.

Suggested Discussion Prompts and Activities

- The story takes place in three locations; the grasslands, the forest, and inside the black river. Which setting is your favorite? Explain.

- Water is one of the five elements in the Chinese Zodiac. Flowing water is *active, aggressive, and restless* while calm water can be *tranquil, silent, and peaceful*. With water's flow of uncertainty, why is it important to always remember think about your feelings and be introspective and reflective?

- How are Shuǐ's qualities similar to qualities of the element of water?

- How does Shuǐ's family feel about her in the beginning and at the end of the story? How do you know this?

- Water bubbles give Shuǐ support and confidence to speak. What are "water bubbles" that help or support you?

- Choose an animal from the Chinese Zodiac and using its character traits, write a story with beginning, middle, and end.

Made in the USA
Las Vegas, NV
29 January 2022